W9-DAL-019

DATE DUE

BY JAKE MADDOX

illustrated by Sean Tiffany

text by Eric Stevens

Librarian Reviewer
Chris Kreie
Media Specialist, Eden Prairie Schools, MN
MS in Information Media, St. Cloud State University, MN

Reading Consultant
Mary Evenson
Middle School Teacher, Edina Public Schools, MN
MA in Education, University of Minnesota

DISCARD

STONE ARCH BOOKS
www.stonearchbooks.com

Impact Books are published by Stone Arch Books
151 Good Counsel Drive, P.O. Box 669
Mankato, Minnesota 56002
www.stonearchbooks.com

Copyright © 2009 by Stone Arch Books

All rights reserved. No part of this publication may be reproduced
in whole or in part, or stored in a retrieval system, or transmitted in any
form or by any means, electronic, mechanical, photocopying, recording,
or otherwise, without written permission of the publisher.

Library of Congress Cataloging-in-Publication Data
Maddox, Jake.
    Lacrosse Attack / by Jake Maddox; illustrated by Sean Tiffany.
    p. cm. — (Impact Books. A Jake Maddox Sports Story)
    ISBN 978-1-4342-0776-0 (library binding: alk. paper)
    ISBN 978-1-4342-0872-9 (pbk.: alk. paper)
    [1. Lacrosse—Fiction. 2. Competition (Psychology)—Fiction.]
I. Tiffany, Sean, ill. II. Title.
PZ7.M25643Lac 2009
[Fic]—dc22   2008004291

Summary: Peter makes the varsity lacrosse team, but one of his
teammates isn't happy about it.

Art Director: Heather Kindseth
Graphic Designer: Kay Fraser

1 2 3 4 5 6 13 12 11 10 09 08

Printed in the United States of America

TABLE OF CONTENTS

DISCARD

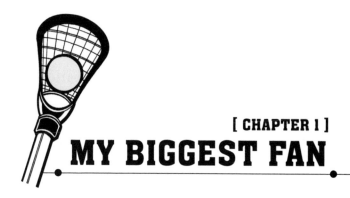

[CHAPTER 1]
MY BIGGEST FAN

It was Sunday afternoon. I was sitting on the edge of the comfy couch in the TV room of my house.

I'd been flipping the remote at lightning speed. I was going back and forth between two channels that most people never even watch.

My friend Eddy's head was hanging upside down next to me. "Peter," she said. "Really. Stop!"

Yes, Eddy is a girl. Her real name is Meredith Parker, but she took the "Ed" from the middle of "Meredith" and made it into "Eddy."

Eddy was sitting on the couch. Her feet were hanging over the back. Her head was where her legs should have been.

She rolled her eyes. "Can you please stop changing the channel for, like, half a second?" she said.

Eddy knows me pretty well. We've been neighbors since we were babies. We grew up together. And she knows that I use the remote control faster and better than anyone.

"Eddy," I replied, "Georgetown is playing Johns Hopkins on channel 122, and Cornell is playing Duke on 183!"

I'd been switching between two big college lacrosse games pretty much nonstop since Eddy had come over an hour earlier. I guess it was making her kind of crazy.

"Well," she said with a big sigh. Then she lifted her head and flipped around to lie on her side for a while. "I guess I can forgive you if it's lacrosse. I mean, you deserve to celebrate. And tomorrow's the big day."

Eddy was right about that. I was celebrating. And that's because last week, I'd become the first ninth grader at River City High School to make it onto the varsity lacrosse team.

Eddy is my biggest fan. When they announced the team on Friday, I thought she was more excited about it than I was.

I don't know why Eddy said tomorrow was the big day, though. I thought the big day was tryouts last week. Tomorrow was just the first day of practice.

What could be exciting about that?

CHAPTER 2

LUNCHTIME LOSER

"So, are you nervous?" Curtis asked the next day.

He and I were sitting in the cafeteria at lunch, poking at the chicken-fried steak on our trays. Well, that's what the lunch lady called it, anyway. It was really a mushy pile of meat on top of a mushy pile of noodles.

It didn't look like steak to me. It looked more like dog food.

I shrugged my shoulders. "A little, I guess," I replied. "Mostly I'm excited to get out there and play."

Lacrosse is my favorite sport by far. I also run track, but I don't love it like I love lacrosse.

Curtis is a lacrosse player too. He didn't make the varsity team, though. I guess he was pretty jealous. The good news for him was he would be the captain of the junior varsity team. That sounded pretty good to me. Besides, the JV captain always gets to start on the varsity team the next year. Everyone knows that.

"Yeah," said Curtis. "I know what you mean. I hope being captain isn't going to mean I can't have fun anymore."

I nodded. "That's what I'm worried about too," I said.

I stabbed at the noodles on my plate, but they were all stuck together. When I tried to pick up just one, the whole clump came off the plate at the same time. "I mean, what if being on varsity is tougher than I think it will be?" I asked. "What if I can't handle it?"

Curtis shook his head. "You'll be fine," he said. "Hey. There's Coach Tory." Curtis pointed to the lunch line.

I turned around. The coach was holding a tray, which was filled with steak, two dishes of Jell-O, a peanut butter and jelly sandwich, three cartons of milk, a salad, a roll, and a huge piece of carrot cake with cream cheese frosting.

"You should go and talk to him," Curtis said. "You're only a freshman. You're going to have to push for field time."

I nodded. "Yeah, you're probably right," I said.

I took one last look at the glob of noodles and dog food on my tray. "I'll be right back," I told Curtis.

I walked over to Coach Tory. He was handing over his money to the cashier at the end of the line when I reached him.

"Coach?" I said. I was too quiet. He didn't hear me. "Coach?" I tried again, a little louder.

"Huh?" the coach said when he finally heard me. It startled him and his tray almost tipped over. Luckily, only one of the milk cartons fell off, and I caught it easily.

"Oh!" Coach said, looking down at me. He's tall. "Nice catch. Peter Stiles, right?" he asked.

"That's right," I replied. "I'm the new freshman on the varsity team."

"I remember," Coach said. "What can I do for you?"

"Well," I said, "I know I'm a freshman, but I was hoping I'd be able to get some real field time this season."

Coach raised his eyebrows at me. "You think you're that good, Stiles?" he asked.

"I guess so, Coach," I said.

I looked at my shoes. I started to worry that it had been a bad idea to talk to him.

He looked down at me, squinted, and said, "First practice is today, so we'll see how you do. But remember, Hurley Johnson is captain, and he's a senior. And he's also an attackman. He will be tough competition for you out there!"

Then Coach Tory walked off. I went back to the table, where Curtis was still playing with his food. "How'd it go?" Curtis asked when I sat down.

"I don't know," I replied. "Hurley is going to be hard to beat for field time."

"Yeah," Curtis said, nodding. "But you can't expect to be the number-one man on offense. Just play good enough to start, and you'll get plenty of time on the field."

I nodded. Just then, I felt a tap on my shoulder. It was Eddy.

"Hi, guys," she said. "Peter, you ready for history class?"

"Yes," I said, sighing. Another lunch hour, over too soon.

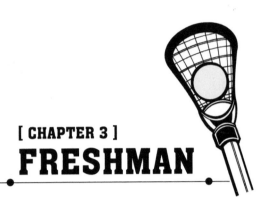

[CHAPTER 3]
FRESHMAN

The guys on the varsity lacrosse team were much bigger than I thought they'd be. Especially Hurley Johnson.

"Hey, freshman!" he said as I walked onto the field.

I was carrying my crosse in one hand, and my helmet in the other. It felt good to wear the varsity uniform, even just to practice.

That is, it felt good until Hurley started picking on me.

"You sure that uniform isn't too big for you?" Hurley teased.

He and another player were tossing a ball back and forth. The other player was as tall as Hurley, but much skinnier. And he threw the ball at Hurley really, really fast.

"Hey, Nick," Hurley said. "You think this freshman can handle varsity lacrosse?"

The other boy laughed. "Not a chance, Hurley!" he said loudly.

That made me pretty mad, but I couldn't start anything with these two.

"Don't worry about them," another player said, standing next to me. "You're Peter Stiles, right?"

I nodded. "That's me," I said.

"I'm Stan Kim," the guy said. "Good job making the team!"

"Thanks," I replied. At least someone was happy to have a freshman on the varsity team.

A sharp whistle blow snapped us all to attention.

"Okay, guys," Coach said when we'd all gathered around him. "We're just going to run some drills today. Everyone, get in line for eagle-eye!" Then he blew another sharp blast on his whistle.

Everyone started getting into groups of six. I looked around. Then I spotted a group of five guys to join.

I was excited. Eagle-eye is my favorite throwing drill.

Players line up, three on three, and toss balls in a pattern among themselves. Sometimes you do the drill with three, four, five, or even six balls to make it harder.

"Let's get going, boys!" Coach called out. Suddenly a ball was coming right at me. I quickly pulled up my crosse, caught the ball, and tossed it off to the guy across from me.

"Listen for my whistle to switch!" Coach warned us. That meant that every time he blew his whistle, the pattern would flip, and the balls would have to be thrown in the other direction.

So far, everything was going pretty well. I was glad Hurley and Nick weren't in my group. I had a feeling Hurley would try to make me mess up, and Nick's throws were so fast, I might have missed one.

After a while, Coach walked around and added a ball to each group. That made it harder, but I kept up.

"Woo! Go Stiles!" I heard. I glanced over to the sideline. Eddy was there, cheering me on. It felt good to see my friend on the sideline.

"Who is that girl?" I heard Hurley say to Nick as he caught a ball and passed it on. "Cheering for the freshman? He's the worst player on the team!"

Nick laughed. He whipped a ball to the next player in their group.

"She should be cheering for me! The captain!" Hurley added. "Look, I'll prove it!"

Suddenly, he caught a ball. He cradled it for a moment, and then whipped it away — right at me!

I saw it coming, but there was no way I could catch it and keep the pattern alive in my own group. One ball was coming from my group. There was one ball in my crosse that I needed to throw on to the next player. And a rocket ball was coming from Hurley. I didn't know what to do.

So I just threw the ball I had. Then I ducked. The ball Hurley had thrown sailed over my head.

Nick laughed. "Nice catch, freshman!" he called over.

"Yeah," called Hurley. "How'd you make this team, anyway?"

CHAPTER 4

HOTSHOT

"I can't believe he did that!" Eddy said. It was Tuesday morning and we were walking to school together. She was still mad about what happened during practice the day before.

"He said it was an accident," I replied. "Coach yelled at him about it. He said if it was an accident, then Hurley needs more ball-control practice. But I don't think it was an accident."

"Me either," Eddy said. "Hey, there he is."

We had just reached the front of the school. Hurley and Nick were hanging out near the front door. When I looked over, I noticed Nick pointing at me. Then Hurley started walking over.

"Oh great," I said. "Here he comes."

"Just keep walking," Eddy said.

Someone grabbed me by the shoulder. "What?" I said, turning around.

It was Coach Tory. "I just wanted to let you know that you did great at practice yesterday," he said with a smile.

"Oh, thanks," I mumbled.

"You must have done eagle-eye before, huh?" he asked with a wink.

"Yes, sir," I said.

"He sure has, Coach," Eddy added. "He's been going to lacrosse camp every summer since he was six!"

"Is that right?" Coach asked. "Well, it shows. Keep it up, Stiles." He walked off.

But Hurley had caught up to us, and he'd heard the whole thing.

"You think you're some kind of hotshot, Stiles?" he said. He gave me a little shove on the shoulder.

"No," I said.

"If I see you trying to kiss up to the coach again, I'll have to do something about it," Hurley said, poking my chest. "You got it?"

"Back off," Eddy said from behind me.

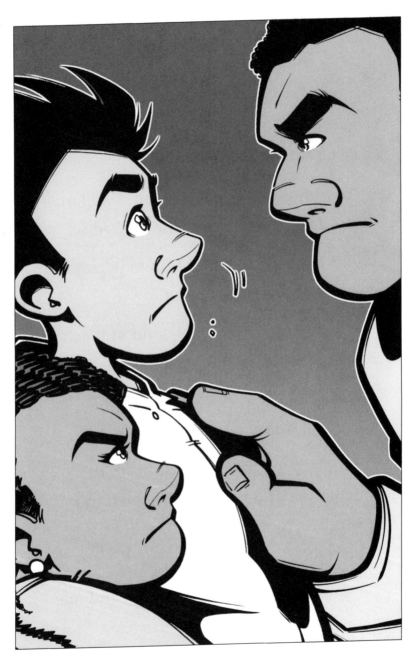

"You're just afraid a freshman is better than you," she added. "It's so obvious."

Hurley glared at Eddy. Then he gave me one more little shove and walked back over to Nick.

"The bell's going to ring any second, Peter," Eddy said, grabbing my hand and pulling me toward the entrance.

But my mind wasn't on homeroom. I was too busy worrying about what would happen during practice that day.

[CHAPTER 5]
SCRIMMAGE

The day went by too fast. That always happens when I'm nervous about something. If I'd been looking forward to practice, the day would have felt like a hundred years.

After school, Curtis and I met in the locker room. We got ready for practice.

"Well, it's a good thing you're on the same team, right?" Curtis said as he pulled on his JV jersey.

Then he went on, "I mean, if Hurley played at a different school, he'd be able to check you all the time. Then he could do some real damage."

"I guess so," I replied. "Of course, if he played at a different school, he probably wouldn't know I existed."

"Good point," Curtis replied. "And good luck." He slammed his locker and left.

I finished getting ready. Then I headed out to the field.

"Okay, guys," Coach said as we gathered around. "I want to start with a scrimmage today."

A scrimmage? That meant Hurley and I could end up on opposite teams. Then he could check me!

"I'll pick the teams today," the coach went on. "I want Peter and Hurley to attack for team A. Nick and Stan will attack for team B."

That was a relief. Hurley wouldn't be able to check me if we were on the same team.

Coach selected the rest of each team. Then Hurley and Stan squatted for the face-off.

Coach placed the ball between them. He backed off and blew his whistle.

The face-off was over pretty fast. Hurley brought in his shoulder and knocked Stan over.

Stan tried to get the ball, but he missed. Then Hurley took control of the ball and started up field.

I was totally open, but Hurley ran the ball up and went for the shot himself. He was a typical ball hog.

But as he got close to the crease, the other team's defense closed in. Stan got back on his feet. He reached his crosse in, stick-checked Hurley, and knocked the ball loose.

Then, quickly, Stan scooped up the ball and looked down the field. In a flash, he made a great pass to Nick.

It was easy for Nick to score. My team's defense didn't have time to react.

Coach blew his whistle to note the goal. Then he blew it again.

"Sidelines, team A," he yelled. We all ran over to the coach while team B threw the ball around.

"Hurley, you should have passed that ball off," Coach Tory said. "We're not out here for glory, all right?"

"Sorry," Hurley said. But he didn't sound like he meant it.

"And, Hurley?" Coach added. "Let's try you on defense. Peter, I want to see you take a strong attack. All right?"

I nodded. "Okay," I said.

"Defense?" Hurley snapped. "I'm the number-one attackman, Coach!"

"Take it easy," Coach replied. "You'll get back on attack later on. But right now I want to see Peter as number one. And you're looking like you might have slowed down a little, Hurley. We'll work on your speed in drills after the scrimmage."

Hurley looked like he might fall over.

I kind of felt the same way. I was the number-one attackman for our scrimmage team!

It was pretty exciting, but it made me worry even more about Hurley's bullying.

"Okay," Coach said, and his clapped his hands. "Play ball. Get out there."

Stan beat me in the face-off, but I didn't let it get to me. He was bigger than I was, and it was my first face-off on varsity. Plus, a few seconds into play, I heard Eddy cheering for me from the sidelines.

"Your dorky friend is back," Hurley said as he ran past me during play. "You better tell her to shut up."

I tried to ignore him. Stan moved toward our goal, but Hurley got to him in time and threw his shoulder into Stan's side.

Stan lost control of the ball and Hurley scooped it up.

"Look out, freshman!" he shouted. Then he whipped the ball right at my head.

I know he was hoping it would hit me, or at least that I'd miss. But I got my crosse up, caught the ball, and took off toward team B's crease.

Goal!

I couldn't believe it. I'd scored my first goal as a varsity player, even if it was just in a scrimmage! Then, the next thing I knew, something slammed into me, and I was flat on my back.

[CHAPTER 6]
HIT BY A TRUCK

I must have blacked out for a second. When I opened my eyes, I saw Coach's face looking down at me. The whole team was gathered around, and Coach was kneeling over me.

"He's all right," he said as I opened my eyes. "Just had the wind knocked out of him. Hurley, have a seat on the bench. Everyone else, get ready for some drills," he ordered.

Coach looked at me and added quietly, "Take your time, Peter. Then hit the showers."

He got to his feet and walked over to Hurley, who was sitting on the bench with his helmet off, looking angry.

Suddenly, Eddy appeared. "Are you okay, Peter?" she asked.

I slowly sat up with a groan. "Yeah, I'm okay," I replied. "I only have one question. Why was someone driving a truck across the lacrosse field?"

"A truck?" Eddy asked, confused. "What are you talking about?"

"Didn't I get hit by a truck?" I asked.

"Oh, ha ha," Eddy said with a smirk. "Something like that. It was Hurley Johnson."

"Hurley checked me?" I asked, surprised. "He was on my team!"

"I know. I saw the whole thing," Eddy said. "He's so jealous of you that he actually checked his own teammate!"

"And after the play was over," I said.

"He should get kicked off the team," Eddy snapped as I got to my feet.

Together, we headed off the field. We headed toward the locker room.

"That will never happen," I replied, shaking my head. "He's the captain. And he's one of the best varsity players in the state."

We stopped outside the boys' locker room. Eddy said, "I heard your coach say that Hurley has slowed down since last season."

"He was moving pretty fast when he slammed into me," I said, rubbing my sore side where Hurley had checked me.

"Hey!" Coach called to me from the field. "I said hit the showers!"

"Yeah," Hurley added. He was still sitting on the bench, and it looked like Coach had been giving him a lecture. "Stop talking to your girlfriend! It's time for your bath! Don't forget your rubber ducky!"

Eddy rolled her eyes. Then she said, "He's such an idiot."

* * *

After Curtis's practice was over, Curtis, Eddy, and I went to my house to watch TV.

"You have to talk to the coach," Curtis said. "That crazy Hurley is going to make ground beef out of you!"

Eddy tossed a pillow at his head. "He's not going to kill you, Peter," she said. "But Curtis is right. You should talk to your coach."

"How will that help?" I asked. "I think I just need to put up with it. He'll stop if I just ignore him."

"You ignored him today," Eddy pointed out. "And you ended up out cold on your back!"

"True," Curtis said.

"But what if I talk to Coach and he thinks I'm just being a baby?" I asked. "What if he thinks I can't handle varsity?"

Curtis and Eddy glanced at each other, then back at me. They both shrugged.

Great, I thought. *Thanks a lot, guys.*

CHAPTER 7

THE THREAT

"Just go talk to him!" Curtis said to me at lunch the next day. "He's in the line!"

Coach was about to pay for his lunch. His tray was stacked with pizza rolls, French fries, three milks, a chocolate pudding, a vanilla pudding, and a bowl of soup.

"I don't know, Curtis," I said. "I think he'll tell me that I can't handle varsity."

"No way, Peter," Curtis replied. "You're too good. Just talk to him."

I let out a big sigh. "Fine, I'll ask him. But if I get bumped down to JV, you have to let me be co-captain."

Curtis laughed. "You got it," he said.

I walked over to Coach just as he was finished paying. "Hi, Peter," he said. "Are you bruised up from that hit you took yesterday?"

"No, Coach," I said. "I'm fine to play."

"Good," Coach said. "Hurley hit you a little late, didn't he?"

Plus, he was on my team! I thought.

Just then, someone grabbed my shoulder. It was Nick. "Excuse us, Coach," he said. "I just need to talk to freshman — I mean, Peter — for a second."

"Okay," Coach replied, walking away. "I'll see you both at practice."

Nick got right in my face. "You kissing up to the coach again?" he growled.

"What?" I said. "No. Not at all!"

"Yeah, you are," Nick said. "And I have a feeling Hurley won't like that."

"Nick," I said, "I'm not! He was just asking me if I had a bruise from yesterday."

"Ohhh," Nick said with a grin. "So you're getting Hurley in trouble and kissing up to the coach!"

"No!" I said, but it was too late.

"I better go talk to Hurley," Nick said as he walked out of the cafeteria. "Say your prayers, freshman!"

I walked slowly back to the table, where Curtis and Eddy were waiting for me. "I have to get out of here!" I said to my friends.

"Out of here?" Curtis said. "One problem, Peter. Classes! You have to, you know, go to them!"

"Yeah, and history class starts in about two minutes," Eddy pointed out.

"Classes?" I said. "I don't care about classes! Hurley's going to crush me into ground beef! They'll probably serve me for lunch next Monday!"

Curtis laughed.

Eddy shook her head. "Let's get to class, Peter," she said. "We're watching a video. You can hide in the dark."

CHAPTER 8

VARSITY TRADITION

I knew I couldn't really leave school. My attendance needed to be pretty close to perfect to stay on varsity. Then again, maybe staying on varsity lacrosse wasn't the best idea.

"Maybe I should just quit," I whispered to Eddy.

We were sitting way at the back of the class. The teacher was showing us a video about Ancient Greece.

"Quit?" Eddy said back. "Quit what?"

"Quit varsity lacrosse!" I hissed back. "I'll just join Curtis on JV, and next year, when Hurley is gone, I can be on varsity again."

"No way, Peter!" Eddy said. She is my biggest fan, after all. "The first game is tomorrow, and you're obviously the best attackman on the team," she added.

"No way," I said.

"Yes way," Eddy replied. "I watched the whole practice yesterday before Hurley knocked you out."

"You watched the whole practice?" I asked.

"Yes, and it's obvious that Hurley is jealous of your skills," Eddy explained. "That's how I know you're the best."

"What about Stan?" I said. "He's quick, and he's a great player."

Eddy shrugged. "Look, you just can't quit, okay?" she said.

* * *

At practice that afternoon, Coach chose Hurley and me to be scrimmage team captains. "And I'm not getting involved in team selection, plays, positions, or anything," Coach said. "Hurley, Peter, you'll need to select players and assign positions, okay?"

Hurley and I nodded. "I get Nick," Hurley said right away.

I shrugged. "Sounds good," I said. Then I called Stan.

We kept choosing teams like that. Then we assigned positions.

"Stan, you better take number one attack," I said. "You'll be our lead scorer."

"Um," Stan said, "I don't think so, Peter. It's kind of a tradition on varsity."

"A tradition?" I asked.

Stan put his finger to his lips. He pointed at the other team's huddle.

"Listen," he said.

Then I overheard Nick talking to Hurley. "This is the big scrimmage, Hurley," he said. "Coach picked you against the freshman. That means the captain of the winning team is going to be lead attackman at the opening game tomorrow."

"I know!" Hurley snapped. "Do you think I forgot last year?"

I had to admit, Hurley did seem kind of worried. I smiled.

"See?" Stan said to me. "Coach is going to want to see you on lead attack today, Peter. But don't worry about it. We'll all play our best to make sure our team wins the scrimmage."

"Thanks, Stan," I replied, trying to sound calm.

But I wasn't really calm at all. I was worried. I glanced over at Hurley. He was grinning at me.

I had Stan take the face-off, and he did a great job. Even though Hurley was hanging over the ball, Stan was able to flick it off to the left.

I caught it easily. Then I ran through the other team's defense.

Stan came up on the right and took a pass from me. Then he got checked pretty hard, but he managed to toss the ball back to me.

I was just around the left side of the crease. I snuck the ball through and scored our team's first goal.

Coach blew his whistle. "Nice one, Stiles! Keep it up!" he called.

I looked over at Hurley. He kicked the dirt, looking pretty upset.

After that goal, the game was pretty close. My team was good. But Hurley was a lot faster than he'd been the day before, and Nick's amazing passes were really tough to break up.

By the time the third quarter ended, we were tied at ten goals each.

Eddy had been cheering for my team the whole game. I went over to talk to her during the break.

"This is the toughest game of my life!" I said to her, catching my breath.

"You're playing great, though," Eddy said. She handed me a bottle of water.

"Thanks," I said. "But it might not be enough. And this scrimmage will decide who the main attackman is at tomorrow's game."

"It's going to be you, Peter," she said. "You're the best attackman playing today!"

I shook my head. "I don't know," I said.

"Well, I do," Eddy said. She had a twinkle in her eye. "And if I have anything to say about it, you'll definitely start tomorrow!"

[CHAPTER 9]
"YOU'LL BE SORRY!"

The fourth quarter started up with Stan facing off against Nick. I guess Hurley wanted to be able to take the pass, so he could try to score right away.

But too bad for Hurley. Stan won the face-off and flipped the ball out to me. After some pretty nice passes, Stan took a shot on goal, but it was blocked.

Soon, Hurley and Nick were moving toward our goal.

Suddenly Eddy was screaming madly from the stands. "Go, Peter! Wooo, Peter Stiles! Number-one attackman on varsity!" she hollered.

Hurley glared at Eddy. "I'm open, Nick!" he shouted.

But when Nick shot the ball over, Hurley fumbled it a little, and one of our defensemen was able to snatch it away. I heard Hurley growling as Stan and I moved toward his goal.

Soon the score was eleven to ten. My team was ahead.

Eddy went insane, even though Stan was the guy who had really scored the goal. "Wooo, Peter!" she shouted, jumping around like a crazy cheerleader. "Peter's team is the best!"

Hurley ran right over to me before the face-off. "You better tell your friend to shut up," he growled. "This isn't even a real game. Who cheers at a scrimmage? Tell her to shut up or you'll both be sorry. I mean it, freshman."

Nick won the next face-off, and Hurley came charging up the field. I moved fast. I knew better than to get in his way when he was mad.

He got around our defense, with a nice pass to Nick. Then he put up his crosse. "Here, Nick!" he called.

Nick zipped the ball right at Hurley. It was a perfect pass. But just as Nick let go of the ball, Eddy started yelling again.

"Go, Peter!" she yelled. "Stiles is the man!"

Hurley looked over at her angrily. Just then, the ball was reaching his crosse.

Since his eyes were off that rocket-fast pass of Nick's, he missed the catch! The ball went flying out of bounds.

Coach blew his whistle. "Eye on the ball, Hurley!" he shouted.

Eddy kept it up, and Hurley got angrier and angrier. Even though he wasn't on defense, he was paying more attention to trying to check me than he was to trying to score. And he was too busy glaring at Eddy to watch the ball!

Soon my team was up by five goals. We were playing hard. It was really good.

By the time the game ended, I could tell that Nick and Coach were losing patience with Hurley.

As the last few seconds ran off the clock, Coach blew his whistle.

"That's game!" he called out. "Today's winner is Team Stiles."

The whole team jogged over to the benches and pulled off their helmets. Hurley's face was really red. I couldn't tell if it was from the heat in his helmet or if he was about to explode with anger.

Stan smiled at me and gave me a thumbs-up. I smiled back. I felt great!

"Peter, great job out there," Coach said. "You'll be starting on attack at tomorrow's opening game, and you'll be our main guy on offense. Stan, you'll be our second attackman."

"What?" Hurley barked. "A freshman starting?" His face got even redder.

Coach picked up his clipboard.

"Everyone, hit the showers," he said.

"Except you, Hurley. We need to talk about your attitude."

CHAPTER 10

HELP FROM EDDY

After my shower, I headed out of the locker room. Eddy and Curtis were waiting for me.

"Woo, Peter!" Eddy shouted. "Stiles is number one!"

"Okay, okay," I said with a chuckle. "You can stop now. Hurley's not here."

"Man," said Curtis, patting me on the shoulder. "I heard you played great today."

"Thanks," I said. "But I owe a lot to Eddy."

"To Eddy?" Curtis asked. "I heard Hurley Johnson was really careless. You owe a lot to him! I'm confused. What does Eddy have to do with this?"

Eddy smiled. "Peter, you explain it," she said.

"Well," I explained as we walked, "the game had been pretty tight, and Hurley was playing his best. But at one point, Coach called out a compliment to me, and Hurley got mad."

"Right," Eddy said. "So I thought, what if someone was cheering for Peter the whole fourth quarter, like, nonstop?"

"It would drive him crazy!" Curtis answered.

"Now you got it," I said. "With Eddy screaming my name over and over, Hurley got so angry and careless, his team didn't score again."

"Then Peter and Stan Kim took over from there," Eddy added.

"Nice one, guys," Curtis said. The three of us walked on toward my house to watch some TV.

I needed to rest up, after all. I was about to become the first-ever freshman varsity starter at River City High School.

ABOUT THE AUTHOR

Eric Stevens lives in St. Paul, Minnesota. He is studying to become a middle-school English teacher. Some of his favorite things include pizza, playing video games, watching cooking shows on TV, riding his bike, and trying new restaurants. Some of his least favorite things include olives and shoveling snow.

ABOUT THE ILLUSTRATOR

When Sean Tiffany was growing up, he lived on a small island off the coast of Maine. Every day, from sixth grade until he graduated from high school, he had to take a boat to get to school. When Sean isn't working on his art, he works on a multimedia project called "OilCan Drive," which combines music and art. He has a pet cactus named Jim.

GLOSSARY

attendance (uh-TEND-dinss)—when you have perfect attendance at practice, you have not missed one day of practice

cashier (ka-SHEER)—someone who takes in or pays out money

competition (kom-puh-TISH-uhn)—a situation in which two or more people are trying to get the same thing

damage (DAM-ij)—the harm that something does

main (MAYN)—the most important

nonstop (NON-STOP)—without any stops or breaks

obvious (OB-vee-uhss)—easy to see or understand

patience (PAY-shuhnss)—the ability to put up with problems without getting upset

tough (TUFF)—hard or difficult

tradition (truh-DISH-uhn)—something that is always done the same way

LACROSSE WORDS

- **attackman** (uh-TAK-man)—the player who scores goals. The attackmen usually play on the offensive side of the field.

- **check** (CHEK)—to make physical contact with a player on the opposing team. To **stick check** is to check by using one's crosse to make contact.

- **crease** (KREESS)—the circle painted around the goal. Players from the opposing team are not allowed into the crease; if they enter the crease, they receive a technical foul.

- **crosse** (KRAWSS)—the stick used to play lacrosse. The stick has a net on one end, which helps the player catch and throw the ball.

- **drills** (DRILZ)—a way to practice something, by doing it over and over

YOU SHOULD KNOW

- **face-off** (FAYSS-awf)—the first play for the ball to decide which team will control the beginning of the game

- **offense** (AW-fenss)—the team that is attacking or trying to score

- **out of bounds** (OUT UHV BOUNDZ)—out of the field of play

- **quarter** (KWOR-tur)—one of four parts that make up a lacrosse game

- **scrimmage** (SKRIM-ij)—a game played for practice, usually between members of the same team

- **sideline** (SIDE-line)—the line that marks the side boundary of the playing area on a field or court in sports

- **starter** (STAR-tur)—one of the players who begins the game

DISCUSSION QUESTIONS

1. Eddy helps Peter out by making Hurley mad during the scrimmage. Do you think she did the right thing?

2. When Hurley was bullying Peter, was there something that Peter could have done to make the bullying stop?

3. Why didn't Hurley like Peter? Talk about the reasons. Were any of his reasons good ones?

WRITING PROMPTS

1. At the end of this book, Peter finds out that he'll be the starting attackman for his team. What do you think happens in the team's first real game? Write a chapter that explains what happens.

2. Sometimes it can be interesting to think about a story from another character's point of view. Try writing chapter 9 (on page 55) from Hurley's point of view. What does he see? What does he think about? Is his experience the same as Peter's, or different?

3. Have you ever tried out for a sports team? Write about what happened.

— • — INTERNET SITES — • —

Do you want to know more about subjects related to this book? Or are you interested in learning about other topics? Then check out FactHound, a fun, easy way to find Internet sites.

Our investigative staff has already sniffed out great sites for you!

Here's how to use FactHound:

1. Visit *www.facthound.com*

2. Select your grade level.

3. To learn more about subjects related to this book, type in the book's ISBN number: **9781434207760**.

4. Click the **Fetch It** button.

FactHound will fetch the best Internet sites for you!